D0605630
95

 Published in the United States by Golden Books, an imprint of Random House Children's Books, a division of Penguin Random House LLC, 1745 Broadway, New York, NY 10019, and in Canada by Penguin Random House Canada Limited, Toronto, in conjunction with Disney Enterprises, Inc. Golden Books, A Golden Book, A Big Golden Book, the G colophon, and the distinctive gold spine are registered trademarks of Penguin Random House LLC.

randomhousekids.com

ISBN 978-0-7364-3674-8

Printed in the United States of America

10 9 8 7 6 5 4 3 2 1

Adapted by
Bill Scollon

Illustrated by
the Disney Storybook Art Team

A GOLDEN BOOK • NEW YORK

In the first Piston Cup race of the season, the undisputed champion, **Lightning McQueen,** was tearing up the track! His friends Bobby Swift, Cal Weathers, and Brick Yardley were right behind him.

But when the checkered flag came down, it was Lightning McQueen **for the win**!

VROOOM
MOTOR SPEEDWAY
OF THE SOUT
RUSTEZE
95
RUSTEZE
DINOCO
42
octane gain
TURBO VITAMINS

Lightning continued to race hard throughout the season. But one day,

a rookie racer

surprised everyone in his first Piston Cup competition.

The rookie blew past Lightning to take first place. "Whoa!" said Lightning. "Who is that?"

"That's **Jackson Storm,**" replied Bobby.

After the race, Lightning congratulated Storm.

The young racer smirked. "You have no idea what a pleasure it is to finally beat you," he said.

"Thanks!" said Lightning. "Hang on. Did you say 'meet' or 'beat'?"

"I think you heard me," said Storm.

Jackson Storm was the best of the next generation of racers. The **Next Gens** were faster and more efficient than the veteran race cars. They trained on the newest technology and relied on analysis of advanced data, such as weight distribution and aerodynamics, to give them the advantage on the track.

In the following races, Storm won **again and again**.

Many of the veteran racers retired or got replaced. They thought they could never be as fast as the Next Gens.

Lightning refused to retire. In the season's final race, he put everything he had into beating Storm.

Coming out of his final pit stop, Lightning gained the lead. But seconds later, Storm passed him. Lightning pushed himself harder, until—**SCREECH!**—he lost control! Sally and the fans gasped! Lightning spun around and

FLIPPED OVER AND OVER.

Then he finally came to a stop.

SH
95
RUSTEZE

Exhaust
FINAL
ASH!
HORNET
SEASON
Season Ender Fender Bender
Puts Young Hornet In Garage

It took four months for Lightning to recover. With the new racing season just two weeks away, no one knew if he'd ever compete again.

Lightning watched films of his mentor and crew chief, **Doc Hudson**. Doc had suffered a bad crash that ended his career. Lightning didn't want that to happen to him. "I decide when I'm done," he told Sally and Mater. "I need to talk to Rusty and Dusty." He was ready to leave Doc's garage, get a new paint job, and start training.

Rusty and Dusty were Lightning's sponsors and the owners of Rust-eze. They had a big surprise for Number 95—**a new training center**! It had all the best technology: treadmills, virtual reality, and a state-of-the-art **racing simulator**.

Lightning looked around in awe. "Guys, how did you ever do this?" he asked.

"We sold Rust-eze!" Rusty and Dusty announced.

"We just realized you needed something we couldn't give you," Dusty said. They sold Rust-eze to a wealthy business car named Sterling, who could help Lightning get back in the game.

"Welcome to the **Rust-eze Racing Center**!" said Sterling. "I've been a fan of yours forever. And now to be your sponsor? How great is that?"

MPH
193
RPM
RATIO
LOG

After Lightning got a new look, Sterling brought Lightning to the racing simulator. Lightning watched in awe as a yellow car sped on the simulator like a professional.

"Who's the racer?" he asked.

"No, no, no. She's a trainer," said Sterling. "**Cruz Ramirez,** the best trainer in the business."

When Cruz saw Lightning, she wasn't impressed. "He's obviously an imposter," she said. "He looks old and broken-down, with flabby tires."

"Hey!" said Lightning. **"I do not!"**

"Use that!" shouted Cruz.

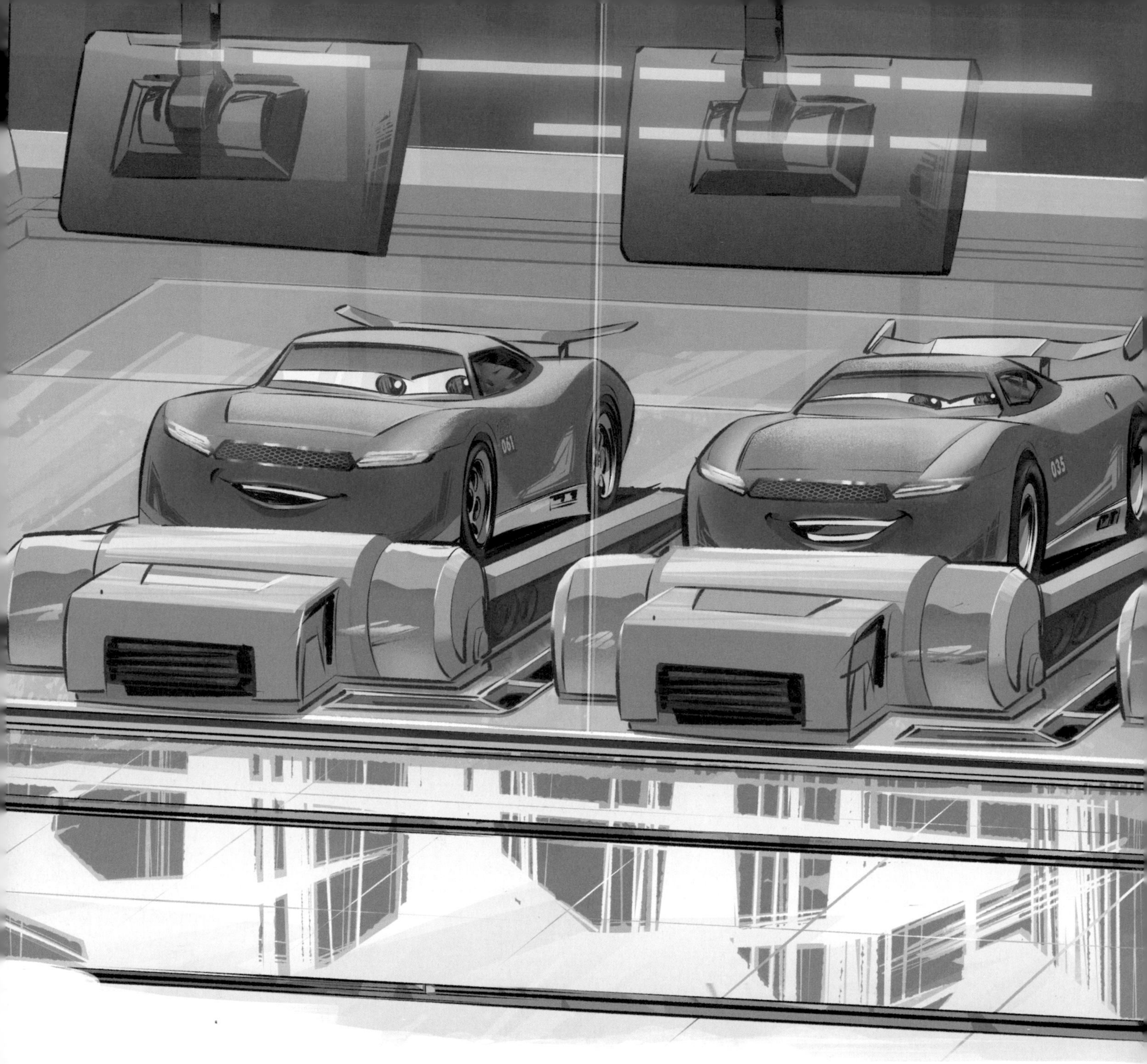

Cruz started Lightning out with an aerobics class. "We need to loosen those ancient joints. First the wheels!

Forward and rest.
Forward and rest!"

Then Cruz challenged Lightning on the treadmill.

"This thing's only going five miles per hour!" Lightning complained.

"We'll work up to the higher speeds," said Cruz. "Right after you take your nap."

After a few days, Sterling decided that Lightning would not compete in the new racing season. "Your speed and performance aren't where they need to be. I'm sorry."

Lightning knew he would never get faster by training with technology. **"I'll train like I did with Doc!"** he said. "I'll get my tires dirty on every dirt track from here to Florida." He promised that with this training, he would beat Storm.

Sterling made a deal with Lightning: if Lightning lost the Florida 500, he would retire and promote the Number 95 brand. If he won, he could continue racing.

Lightning agreed, and soon he was zooming down Fireball Beach. Cruz tried to track Lightning's speed by racing alongside him, but she kept getting stuck in the sand.

"The beach ate me," she said.

By the end of the day, Lightning had taught Cruz how to race on sand. She was finally able to track his speed.

"You're still slower than Storm," said Cruz.

Welcome to...
THUNDER HOLLOW
Speedway
ENTRANCE

Lightning saw a sign nearby for **Thunder Hollow Speedway**. "That's what I need—to race against actual racers," he said.

Mack brought Lightning and Cruz to the track. Then Lightning put on a muddy disguise and signed up for the next race. He had no idea it was a special event: the **Thunder Hollow Crazy Eight demolition derby**!

A crew member painted a number on Cruz's side. "I shouldn't be out here!" she exclaimed. But the gate was locked—Lightning and Cruz would have to compete!

Banged-up vehicles of all kinds tried to knock each other out of the competition. The undefeated champion, a fierce school bus named **Miss Fritter,** took aim at Lightning and Cruz. "Your license plates are gonna look real nice in my collection," Miss Fritter said.

Lightning helped Cruz survive the race. Cruz even won! But Lightning was angry. "I can't get any faster because I'm too busy taking care of my trainer!" he exclaimed. "This is my last chance, Cruz! If I lose, I never get to do this again. If you were a racer, you'd know what I'm talking about."

Cruz was hurt. **"I've wanted to become a racer forever because of you!"** she said. When she had gotten her first chance to race, she thought the other racers were bigger, stronger, and more confident than she was. "I just left. It was my one shot, and I didn't take it." She became a trainer instead.

Cruz decided to return to the training center. After she left, Lightning called Mater and admitted that things weren't going well.

Mater knew Lightning missed getting advice from Doc. "There weren't nobody smarter than old Doc. Except for maybe whoever taught him."

That gave Lightning an idea. **"Smokey! Mater, you're brilliant!"**

The next morning, Lightning caught up to Cruz and apologized for getting upset. He told her he knew someone who could help.

Mack drove them to **Thomasville Speedway**. They saw a sign that read **"Welcome to Thomasville! Home of the Fabulous Hudson Hornet!"** They had arrived at Doc Hudson's home track!

"Want to check out the track of the greatest racer of all time?" Lightning asked Cruz.

The two friends sped around the course. As they came around the curve, they saw someone on the track. It was Doc Hudson's old crew chief, **Smokey**!

Smokey led Lightning and Cruz to a local hangout called the Cotter Pin. Some of the **greatest racers** who ever lived were there. They were known as the **Legends**.

"River Scott," Lightning told Cruz. "Junior 'Midnight' Moon, Louise 'Barnstormer' Nash. They all raced with Doc."

The Legends told Lightning and Cruz about their friend Hud, the **Fabulous Hudson Hornet**.

"Hud was the fastest racer this side of the Mississippi," said River Scott.

"Until he wasn't," added Smokey. "Everything changed when the rookie showed up."

In one race, Hud challenged the rookie for first place and got slammed into the wall.

"Hud knew he couldn't outrun him," Smokey said. "He'd have to **outthink him**."

The Fabulous Hudson Hornet used the wall to launch himself into the air and **flip** over the rookie. He came down in first place!

SERVICE
34
94

Smokey agreed to train Lightning, but Number 95 needed to understand something. "**You're old.** Accept it," Smokey said. "You'll never be as fast as Storm. But you can be smarter."

To help motivate Lightning, Cruz would stand in for Storm. The Legends turned Cruz into a race car—she even got a 2.0 on her side, just like Storm. "You're goin' down, Lightning McQueen!" she said.

Smokey hooked Lightning and Cruz to heavy trailers. "You ain't gonna pass Storm movin' like that!" he shouted. "**Let's go!**"

To test Lightning's handling skills, Smokey let a herd of tractors onto a field. **"Sneak through the window!"** he yelled as Lightning and Cruz tried to weave through the tractors.

Lightning was feeling better than ever as the first race of the new season drew near. Lightning and Cruz took one last practice run around the Thomasville track. Cruz hit the gas and pulled away from Lightning! He gave it all he had—but **he couldn't catch up**.

Everyone was speechless. They didn't know if Lightning could win in Florida. But there was no more time to train—Lightning needed to leave. "I want to thank everyone for the training," he said. He rolled into Mack's trailer and set out for the race.

The sellout crowd at the Florida 500 was electric. When the green flag dropped, Lightning raced hard, passing cars left and right.

"Not too shabby!" Smokey exclaimed. He had come to Florida to be Lightning's crew chief.

Over his headset, Lightning heard Sterling telling Cruz to return to the racing center.

"You're a trainer, remember? Not a racer!" he shouted.

Suddenly, Lightning remembered all his training with Cruz. She deserved to fulfill her dream of becoming a racer.

At that moment, there was a crash on the track. Lightning dodged the wreck and headed back to the pit.

"Smokey! I need Cruz!"

he shouted over the headset.

RUSTEZE
95
RUSTEZE

When Lightning entered the pit, Cruz was waiting for him. "What's going on?" she asked.

"Come on, guys! Get her set up!"

Lightning said to his pit crew. "Hey, Ramone! You got your paints?"

Before Cruz could say anything, Guido changed her tires and Ramone painted the number 95 on her sides. Cruz would finish the race!

"Why are you doing this?" Cruz asked Lightning. "You said it yourself—this might be your last chance."

"Which makes it **my last chance to give you your first chance,**" Lightning replied. "And this time I want you to take it."

54

Cruz zoomed onto the track. When she reached the pack of racers, she was so nervous that she slowed down.

"Come on! Pick it up!" yelled Smokey.

"Tell her the school bus of death is after her!" Lightning said.

Cruz smiled and sped up. Eventually, Lightning took over for Smokey on the crew chief stand. He reminded Cruz about Thomasville. **"Sneak through the window!"**

Cruz visualized the tractors from her training. She found an opening and weaved through the racers. The crowd went wild for this exciting new competitor.

Finally, Cruz caught up to the lead racer—Jackson Storm! Storm was shocked to see her racing next to him, but he wasn't about to let her pass. "I don't think so!" he shouted. Then he slammed Cruz into the wall!

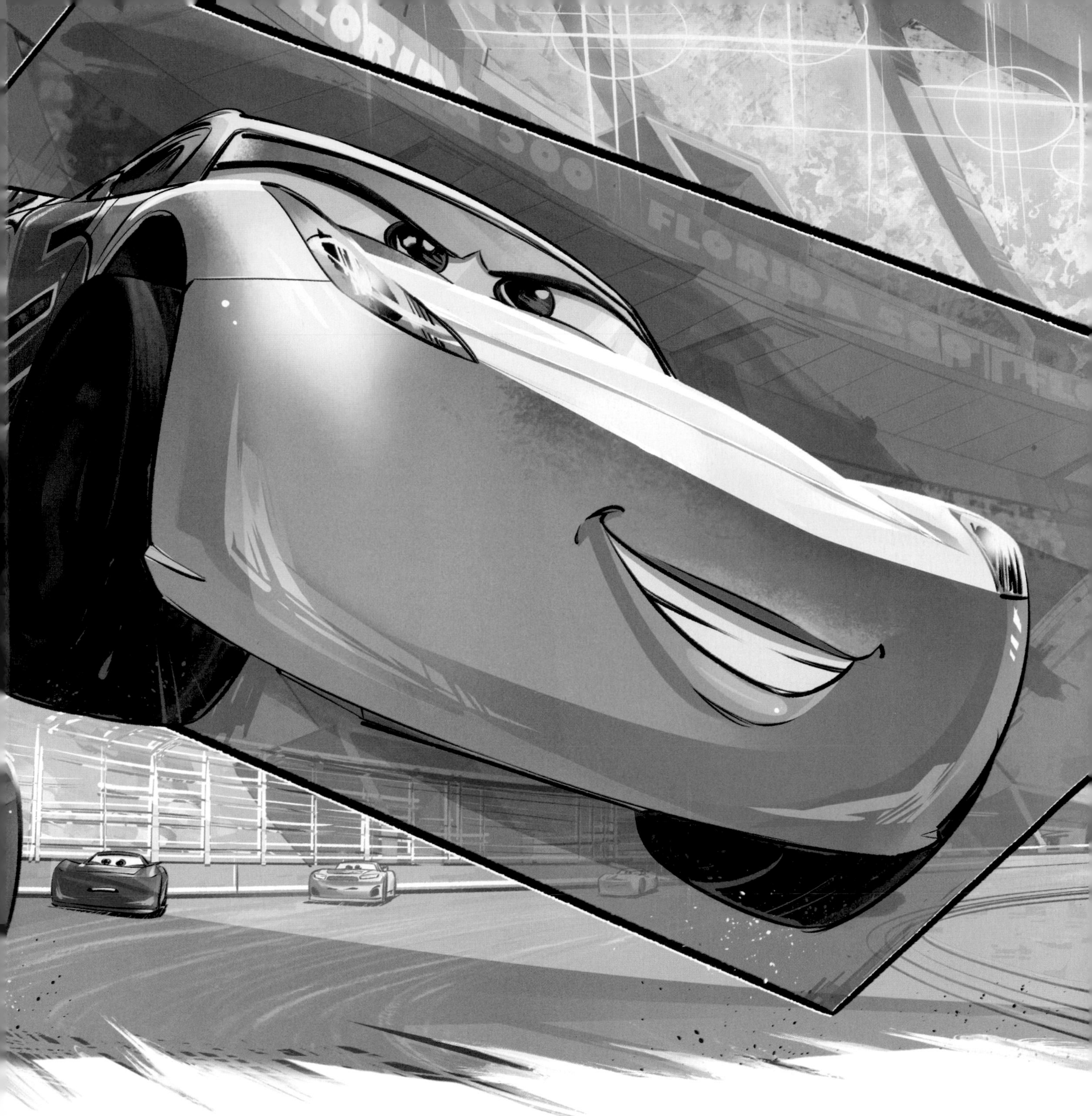

But Cruz stayed calm and remembered Doc's old racing trick. She turned her wheels into the wall, shot into the air, and flipped over Storm! She sped across the finish line as the crowd cheered.

Cruz won the race!

After the race, Sterling asked Cruz to join his team. Cruz quit instead—she would never race for Sterling after the way he treated her. Tex, the owner of Dinoco, overheard Cruz and offered her a racing sponsorship with Dinoco.

Lightning was surprised to learn that he and Cruz had both won! **Lightning had started the race and Cruz had finished it.** He could continue racing and didn't have to work for Sterling.

Back in Radiator Springs, Cruz showed off her new number: Doc Hudson's 51. She was an official race car!

Lightning had a new look, too. He was decked out in blue paint—just like Doc. He was able to keep his number 95 after Tex bought Rust-eze from Sterling. Lightning's racing days weren't over yet! But for now, he focused on getting Cruz ready for the rest of the season.

Cruz couldn't wait to begin. "Bring it on, old man!" she cheered.

Lightning and Cruz zoomed off and raced around Willys Butte, ready to **work together** as a team.

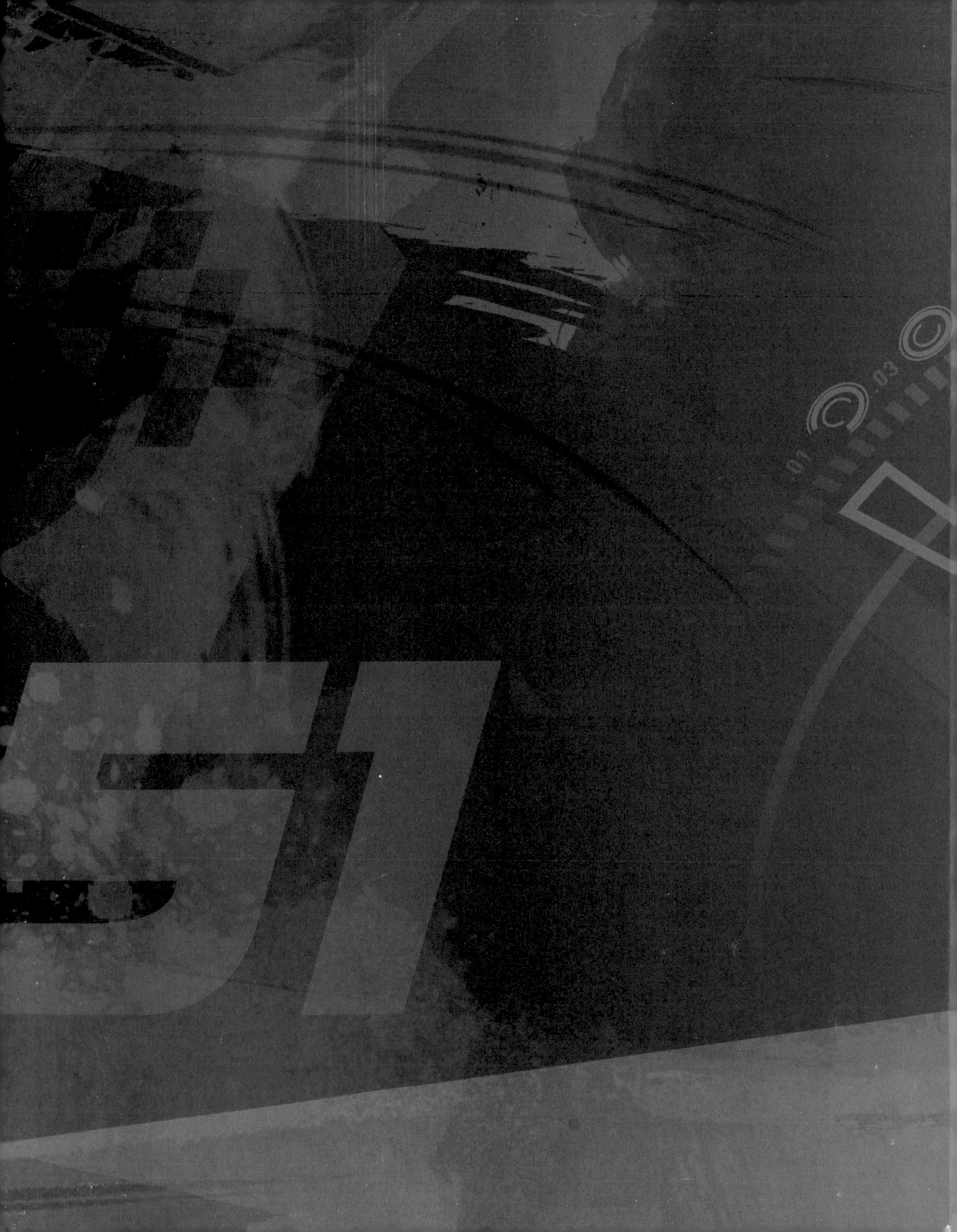